The Thanksgiving Door

DEBBY ATWELL

Houghton Mifflin Company Boston 2003

Walter Lorraine Books

For Ann Tobias and the Women's Bulgarian Choir of Maine —
with thanksgiving

Walter Lorraine ✑ Books

Copyright © 2003 by Debby Atwell

All rights reserved. For information about permission
to reproduce selections from this book, write to
Permissions, Houghton Mifflin Company,
215 Park Avenue South, New York, New York 10003.

www.houghtonmifflinbooks.com

Library of Congress Cataloging-in-Publication Data

Atwell, Debby.
The Thanksgiving door / by Debby Atwell.
p. cm.
Summary: After burning their Thanksgiving dinner, Ann and Ed head
for the local café, where they are welcomed by an immigrant family into an
unusual celebration that gives everyone cause to be thankful.
ISBN 0-618-24036-5
[1. Thanksgiving Day—Fiction. 2. Immigrants—Fiction.] I. Title.
PZ7.A8935 Th 2002
[E]—dc21
2002000414

Printed in Singapore
TWP 10 9 8 7 6 5 4 3 2 1

The Thanksgiving Door

Thanksgiving Day.
Ed and Ann were home alone.
And then — oh no! — Ann burned the dinner.

Ann felt plain awful because she had ruined Thanksgiving.
She decided that she had to iron clothes, but Ed was hungry.
"Let's go see if that new restaurant down the street is open," Ed said.
"Oh, all right," said Ann, "but it won't be the same."

The door to the New World Café was open.

"Hurray," said Ed. He quickly hung up their coats.

Ann said, "Is this a Thanksgiving table decoration? This looks like a Pilgrim and an Indian, but who is the dancing man with the beard?

I'm not sure that we should be here, Ed."

"Nonsense," replied Ed. "Their door was open."

Many unhappy eyes peered through the kitchen door. "This is horrible!" Leon whispered. "Who left the front door open? We can't have customers today! Our party will be ruined."

"Let's get rid of them," said Tatyana. I'll bang these pots together. The noise will scare them away."

Grandmother had heard all that she could bear. She dropped her peeled potato into the pot and said, "Enough! In old country we bang pots at wolves, not hungry people. Today is Thanksgiving Day. Family cooks turkey big as a doghouse, but we don't share? Bah!" She shook her head.

"Grandmother is right," said Olga. "Go get some chairs."
Olga showed Ann and Ed to the best seats at the table.
Aunt Sophia brought two more table settings.
Grandmother said, "Happy Thanksgiving. Welcome,
welcome. We are glad that you are here."

And that's how Ann and Ed found themselves guests
of honor as this family celebrated their first Thanksgiving
in the New World Café.

After dinner Ed asked for a check, but everyone pretended
not to understand.
"No, no, no. We dance now! Please stay."
Ann and Ed had never heard of a family dancing on Thanksgiving,
but they were having such a good time, they just said yes. Ed
followed the men upstairs to help move tables out of the way. Ann
stayed with the women and got to hold the new baby, Sonia.

Uncle Karl struck up the band, and the young dancers got things started. Soon everyone joined in. Even Ed, who had never danced a lick in his life, kicked up his heels.

Ann loved to dance. She knew all of the steps. She taught everyone the conga. In no time at all they were dancing in one huge conga line. What a hit!

It was really late when Ann and Ed said their goodbyes. Grandmother gave Ann a table decoration. Papa and Ed traded hats. Ann gave her telephone number to Sonia's mother, in case she ever needed a babysitter.

They all said, "Thank you for making this such a very special Thanksgiving."

When it was time to lock up the café, Papa could not get the front door to close. When he looked down he found a raw potato jammed under the door.

"How did that stupid thing get there?" he asked.

"In old country Thanksgiving door is like happy heart, opened up big and wide. Potato good for that," Grandmother said.

"You're right" was all Papa said.

When they got home Ann lit the candle from the café and made tea.
"What are you most thankful for on this wonderful Thanksgiving?" she asked.
Ed thought. Many things crossed his mind, but what was he most thankful for?
"Well," he said, "I guess I'd have to say, my dear, that I'm most
thankful that you burned our dinner."
"Oh, Ed," she said, "me too."